BLUE DAISY

BLUE DAISY

Helen Frost

Pictures by
Rob Shepperson

MARGARET FERGUSON BOOKS
HOLIDAY HOUSE · NEW YORK

Margaret Ferguson Books
Text copyright © 2020 by Helen Frost
Illustrations copyright © 2020 by Rob Shepperson
All Rights Reserved
HOLIDAY HOUSE is registered in the U.S. Patent and Trademark Office.
Printed and bound in August 2021 at Maple Press, York, PA, USA.
www.holidayhouse.com
First hardcover edition, 2020
First paperback edition, 2021
3 5 7 9 10 8 6 4 2

Library of Congress Cataloging-in-Publication Data
Names: Frost, Helen, 1949– author.
Title: Blue Daisy / Helen Frost.
Description: First edition. | New York : Margaret Ferguson Books,
Holiday House, [2020] | Summary: Friends Sam and Katie try to help
a stray dog and, in the process, bring their neighbors closer together.
Includes a recipe for dog biscuits.
Identifiers: LCCN 2018041870 | ISBN 9780823444144 (hardcover)
Subjects: | CYAC: Dogs—Fiction. | Animal rescue—Fiction.
Neighbors—Fiction. | Friendship—Fiction.
Classification: LCC PZ7.F9205 Blu 2020 | DDC [Fic]—dc23
LC record available at https://lccn.loc.gov/2018041870

ISBN: 978-0-8234-4414-4 (hardcover)
ISBN: 978-0-8234-4993-4 (paperback)

To seven-year-old Lloyd

BLUE DAISY

THAT DOG

In a time and place where everyone knows
who's home, who's not, who comes and goes,
who's passing through, who's here to stay—
a dog shows up one summer day.

LET'S FOLLOW IT

SAM

I've never seen that dog before.
It walks through Katie's yard to mine
just as I open my back door.

Katie must have seen it too—
here she comes. *Hey, Sam*, she yells,
I don't know that dog. Do you?

I shake my head. *Let's follow it*, I say.
It turns a corner, disappears. *Over there*,
says Katie, pointing. We head that way.

It's sure skinny. I wonder where
it came from. *Does it have a collar?*
I ask Katie. We can't tell from here,

so I say, *Let's get closer.* Katie agrees.
But not too *close*, she says. *That poor
dog is filthy. It probably has fleas.*

WHOSE DOG IS THAT?

KATIE

Sam and I are following the dog when it goes into the Wilson sisters' flower garden before we have a chance to warn it about them.

Uh-oh—it starts digging. The two sisters come charging out.

Shoo! Scram! yells short Ms. Wilson.

Whose dog is that? her taller sister shouts.

The dog runs back and forth between the two of them.

Git out of there, you ugly mutt. Quit that digging! Stop trampling our impatience! They're both so mad by now, I don't know who yells what.

If you ask me, I whisper to Sam, *those two never had much patience to begin with. Let's go.*

Tall Ms. Wilson shakes her broom at that poor skinny dog, which takes off running. It gives Sam and me one quick glance as it goes past.

It's headed toward the park, says Sam. *Come on!*

MEANEST KIDS IN THE WORLD

SAM

Katie thinks we should be taking
the shortcut to the park, to get ahead
of the dog. But this is Mr. Jenkins' baking

day—*he'll have cookies*, I remind her. *Let's stay
here in the alley and see if he's outside.* When we
get near his house, we can tell right away

that he's in a bad mood—he's tossing out
a whole batch of snickerdoodles. Uh-oh—
we're not the only ones who know about

Mr. Jenkins and his cookie-baking habits.
It's Michael and Miranda Tracy—on their
bikes. We turn and run like scared rabbits.

From a distance, Katie glances back. *Sam, look,*
she says. *Michael hopped off his bike
to pick up burned and dirty cookies—he took*

three handfuls! We don't want to be seen
by the Tracy twins—they're the biggest kids
in our grade at school, and they are mean.

Duck behind this garbage can, I say. We
try to hide, but the space is small, so we
scrunch together and peek out. Katie nudges me

and points. *Sam,* she whispers, *that dog turned
around—it's coming this way.* Miranda turns
her bike and chases it. Michael pockets the burned

snickerdoodles, stands up, and throws
something—a rock?—at the dog! Miranda
whizzes by, yelling, *Hey, dog!* She knows

most dogs can't run as fast
as kids ride bikes. I'm pretty sure that dog
is trying to escape. It flashes past

our hiding place and slides
through a hedge. Ha ha—the Tracy twins
can't follow it. Then Miranda rides

straight at our hiding place, and Katie jumps out.
You're the meanest kids in the whole world! she yells.
That dog never did anything to you! I shout.

Miranda swerves around us. *Ooohhh,* she mocks,
meanest kids in the whole world! When she's gone,
I say to Katie, *If that dog could pick up rocks*

and throw them back, I bet it would.
Katie stamps her foot and says, *I'm tempted to do that myself.* Maybe we should.

IT LOOKS HUNGRY

KATIE

Who knows where that dog is now, says Sam. *I'm going home for lunch.*

See you later, I say. As I walk to my house, I keep thinking about the dog.

Who does it belong to? Where did it come from? Why is everyone so mean to it? Is it the dog's fault it's so dirty? What if we gave it a bath? Maybe we can feed it so it won't be so skinny.

Mom, I ask when I get home, *do we have any dog food?*

No, Katie, she says. *Since we don't have a dog, we don't have any dog food.*

I wish we did have a dog, but Mom and I have been through all this before, and her answer is always the same: *No.*

Why are you asking? she wants to know.

There's a dog outside and it looks hungry.

You be careful, Katie. I know you love animals, but a hungry dog might snap at you. Or even bite.

It doesn't look like that kind of dog to me. Even though it's hungry and dirty, I still think it looks nice.

LUCKY FOUR-LEAF CLOVER

SAM

After lunch, Katie wants to look for the dog again,
but Dad wants me to help him paint our old
gray table. *It won't take long,* he promises. *When*

it's done, it will brighten up the kitchen. You
see how scratched up and ugly it is now?
It will look much better, painted blue.

In a sunny spot near some daisies in our yard,
Katie sits and searches for a four-leaf clover
while I help Dad paint. *Hey! That wasn't hard,*

she says. *Look, Sam, I found one! I bet*
it will help us find that dog. Dad sets down his
brush and looks at me. *Sam,* he says, *I can get*

this done myself. Clean your brush, then you two
go find that dog you're worrying about.
I'm sure it could use some friends like you.

HAVE YOU SEEN THAT DOG?

KATIE

Sam and I search everywhere.

We go past the Wilson sisters' house. They're planting a new border, pink and white, where the dog dug up their flowers.

Short Ms. Wilson looks at us and says: *I got some more impatience. You kids better stay out of it! And keep that dog out too!*

Sam says, *Um . . . okay.* And then he asks, *Speaking of that dog, have you seen it?*

No, she answers. *And I don't want to.*

We keep looking. No sign of it anywhere.

We walk by Mr. Jenkins' house again, but he's not outside.

Let's go to his door and say hello, Sam suggests. We knock, and he invites us to come in. We glance around and sniff. It doesn't seem like he made more snickerdoodles—no cookies cooling on his kitchen counter, and there's still a slight burned smell in the air.

I don't want him to think we only came for cookies. *Mr. Jenkins,* I say, *have you seen a dog—walking around all alone, kind of skinny and dirty?*

He nods. *Yes, I saw that dog this morning. And you're not the only ones looking for it. Michael and Miranda Tracy rode by on their bikes about an hour ago and stopped to ask me if I'd seen it.*

Sam glances at me. *Okay, thanks,* he says to Mr. Jenkins, *we'll keep looking.*

Sam, let's try the park, I say. But when we get there, we don't see the dog.

After that, we stop at my house to get a drink of water, and then we walk up the street and down the alley two more times.

Still no sign of the dog.

Maybe it didn't like our neighborhood and went somewhere else.

I wish it would come back and give us another chance.

AN IDEA

SAM

Katie and I end up at my house, discouraged. Dad
has finished painting the tabletop, but not the legs,
and the paint can is under the table in the shade

with the lid beside it. The paintbrush is lying there
unwashed, and I lean down to pick it up. *What?
Katie look! That dog found its way here*

while we were gone! We searched half the day,
all over town, and now we find it here, asleep in my
backyard, in the shade of the painted table. *No way!*

says Katie. Yes. It's true—the dog is fast asleep,
sad and skinny, looking like it needs a friend
or two. We should leave it alone and let it keep

on sleeping. But . . . the paint is so clean. So blue.
I'm holding a paintbrush in my hand. I look
at the sleeping dog. Katie is looking at it too.

A SECOND OR TWO

KATIE

Sam turns the paintbrush over, shifts it to his other hand.

He's staring at the dog.

We look at the table, shining turquoise blue. We look at the skinny, dusty dog.

The can of paint is the color of a swimming pool— and the brush Sam's holding seems to dive right in.

He lifts it out. Looks at me. I'm not sure what he's thinking.

The paint drips back into the can. Sam wipes the brush on the side of the can so it stops dripping, and then he lifts it up again.

He looks back at the dog.

My mind says: *No, Sam. Don't.*

My voice says—nothing.

The dog's eyes are closed. It's breathing up and down. Up. And down. Fast asleep.

Sam does exactly what I don't tell him not to: he runs the brush along the dog's thin back.

A tiny puff of dust. A quiver.

It's only a second or two.

And then a streak of blue shines where before it was all gray.

The dog keeps on sleeping. Breathing up and down.

Sam holds out the brush to me.

A STREAM OF BLUE

SAM

Katie stares at the streak of turquoise shining along
the dog's gray back like a racing stripe.
(Could something that looks so good be wrong?)

Without a word, she accepts the brush
and holds it carefully. It's a little dirty now,
especially compared to the clean, fresh

paint. I move the paint can closer to her. She twirls
the brush above it, dips it in,
lifts it out. A stream of blue curls

back into the can. Katie whispers, *I don't
think I should have done that, Sam.
Look what happened. Your dad won't*

*like finding dirt and dog hair in his blue
paint.* She lifts the brush up in the air,
as if she's not sure what to do.

A drop of paint falls on the dog's fur.
Then three more. Katie and I watch them
splash down, so softly the dog doesn't stir.

At first we're silent. Then: *I could make them into flower petals*, Katie says. We both hesitate. And then I say, *My stripe could be the stem.*

MAYBE. MAYBE NOT.

KATIE

The dog keeps breathing in and out. Up and down. I lean closer. So does Sam.

Using a corner of the brush, I make each drop of paint into a petal and start to make a circle in the center.

It's starting to look a little bit like a blue daisy.

Then the dog wakes up with a jerk. The paintbrush makes a splotch right where the petals meet the stem.

The dog stands up, glances at Sam and me, turns, and runs off down the alley.

Sam and I look around to see if anyone is watching. We don't see anyone.

It doesn't have a collar, I tell Sam.

I know, he answers. *It must not have a home.*

Did someone just abandon it, and leave it on its own? I ask.

Sam shakes his head and says, *What kind of person would do a thing like that?*

And then we both get quiet, thinking about what *we* just did.

Maybe it was dreaming we were petting it with the paintbrush, I say. *It might have liked that feeling.*

Maybe, says Sam. *Maybe not.*

• • •

Sam and I go to my house. When we go in, Mom gives us a funny look.

What? I say.

She squints. *You two look like you've been up to something.*

Who, us? Sam says, all Mister Innocent. We go outside where Mom can't hear us.

What if it tries to lick the paint off? I ask Sam.

Paint might be poison to dogs, he says.

That's exactly what I'm worried about.

How long does it take for paint to dry? he asks.

I don't know, I say. *We should try to get it off before it does.*

But we don't know how to do that, and we can't think of anyone to ask who wouldn't make us tell them why we want to know.

WET OR DRY?

SAM

What's that? *Katie, listen! We're in luck!*
"Pop Goes the Weasel" is jingling on our street.
It's my uncle Jerry and his ice cream truck.

We can ask him about the paint, I say. *Worth a try,*
Katie agrees, so we run over. *Uncle Jerry,* I ask, *how do you
get paint off—something?* He thinks about it. *Wet or dry?*

he wants to know. Katie looks at me. Would it be dry yet?
Where is the dog by now? How will we even find it?
I'm not sure, I answer. *What if it's still wet?*

Uncle Jerry takes his time, first telling
us a story about when he was a kid and he
got paint on his Sunday clothes, his mom yelling

at him and soaking it off with turpentine.
But these days, he says, *most paint is water-based.
Now if I got paint on something of mine,*

I'd use soap and water before it dried on there.
We start to take off running, but Uncle Jerry calls us back.
Don't you two want a Popsicle to share?

DIRT AND DOG HAIR IN THE PAINT

KATIE

We stop just long enough for Uncle Jerry to split an orange Popsicle in half for us, and we eat it on the run. When we get to Sam's house, the dog has returned! It's rolling in the grass—is it trying to get the paint off?

Sam's dad comes out and looks around. *I forgot to put away the paint,* he says. Then he asks, *What happened here? There's dirt and—it looks like dog hair—in the paint! And what's that on the dog? Do you kids know anything about this?*

Sam doesn't answer. I think fast. *Maybe the dog rolled over on the paintbrush,* I suggest. I wish my flower looked more like it was just a blob of blue.

Sam's dad puts the lid back on the paint. *I should have cleaned this up right away,* he says. *I wonder if the paint will hurt that dog.*

That's what we want to know. We wait for him to tell us what he thinks, but he just takes the paint and paintbrush and goes inside.

Sam looks at me. *Maybe it's not completely dry,* he says. *We should try to wash it off. I'll go get some soap and turn on the hose. Katie, see if you can catch the dog.*

But when I take a step toward it, it stands up and glares at me. I don't think it likes me very much.

When I say, *Here, dog,* it turns away.

I wish it had a name.

Here, Duke, I try. *Here, Scamper. Here, Lucky. Here, Pongo. Hey, what are you, anyway—a boy or a girl?*

Did this dog understand me? It squats and pees in the grass, as if to answer, *I'm a girl.*

I try all the girl dog names I know: *Here, Anna. Here, Ruby. Here, Misty. Here, Maya.*

She doesn't even glance my way.

Sam comes back with a bottle of Ivory liquid soap in one hand, dragging the hose in the other. He hands me the soap, turns on the water, and points the hose at the dog. At first, she backs away.

But then Sam starts to jiggle the hose up and down, making the water sparkle in the sunlight. The dog takes a few steps toward Sam and opens her mouth.

Sam, I say, *I think she wants a drink.*

Sam holds the hose still for a minute and the dog comes closer and drinks from it.

See if you can slowly bring the water over this way, I suggest, *so I can squirt some soap on her.*

Very carefully, step-by-step, Sam guides her closer to me. When she's close enough, I squirt soap on her back, and Sam lets the water fall on top of the soap, right on the blue daisy.

BRIGHTER THAN BEFORE

SAM

One small patch of clean fur gives Katie and me hope—
but the daisy is still there, shining brighter than before.
When Katie tries to get closer, to squirt more soap,

the dog turns and runs, without looking back. Why?
I say, *I think we scared it, Katie.* She nods, then says,
The dog is "her," not "it." And that paint must be dry.

WE BREATHE AGAIN

KATIE

Sam and I turn off the hose and go inside.

His dad is talking on his phone: *Say, could you tell me what to do if a dog gets paint on its fur?*

Pause.

Water-based latex.

Pause.

I'm not sure. Could be dry.

Pause.

A thin stripe about as long as my forearm, and a blob as big as my hand. (Did Sam's dad just call my blue daisy a blob?)

We hold our breath while he listens. *Thank you,* he says. And he puts down his phone.

I was talking to a veterinarian, he tells us.

And? We wait.

The dog should be okay, he says.

We breathe again.

Sam's dad shakes his head and says, *It doesn't look to me like that dog rolled over on a paintbrush. It looks like someone painted it on purpose.* He looks at us like he's trying to decide if we're the culprits, but he doesn't actually accuse us.

Whoever it was, he finally says, *they're lucky the dog didn't snap or bite. It must be a very gentle dog.*

I almost say, *Yes, we are* and *I know. It must be.* But I manage to keep quiet.

I better go home now, Sam, I say. *See you tomorrow.*

BLUE DAISY

The dog explores the neighborhood,
sniffing fences, finding food,
splashing through puddles, kicking up dust.
Where is she safe? Who can she trust?

YOU THINK WE'RE MEAN?

SAM

Right after breakfast, Katie comes over.
Sam, she says, *I could hardly sleep last night.*
Remember how I found that four-leaf clover?

I guess it brought good luck to me,
because we did find the dog—but what about
that dog's luck? I feel terrible about what we

did. I know what Katie means. Plus, I hate
how everyone is calling her That Dog. She needs
a name. *Katie*, I say, *let's put water by my gate*

for her. We do that, and then sit on the steps. The first
people we see are the Tracy twins, heading our way.
Being chased down the alley isn't the worst

that happened to that dog, Miranda yells. *Someone got*
paint all over it! Michael adds, *You think* we're *mean?*
Whoever did that is meaner. My face gets hot—

meaner than the Tracy twins? Me? Katie? No!
We're nice. They're the mean ones.
Ask anyone! *C'mon, Katie*, I say, *let's go.*

BOO DAISY

KATIE

Sam and I walk to the park. As soon as we get there, a squirrel starts scolding us. Next, a dog strains at its leash and barks at us. And then a big black bird lands on a park bench and screeches when we walk by.

What if we *are* the meanest kids in the world, and even the birds and animals know it?

Hey! There's the dog! says Sam.

Will she bark at us too? Will she growl if we get too close?

She doesn't do that—she just ignores us and trots over to a mother and her baby. We decide to follow.

The mother says, *I wonder why that dog has a blue daisy on its back.* (She doesn't say "blob," she says "blue daisy"!)

The baby points and says, *Boo Daisy!*

A young man hears the baby say that and repeats it, smiling, first at the baby, then at the dog. He reaches down to pet the dog, calling her Blue Daisy, and Blue Daisy lets him scratch behind her ears.

Blue Daisy? says a young woman walking past. *I was wondering what that dog's name was.* She smiles at the

young man and asks, *Is this your dog?*

The man smiles at her too—everybody's smiling now. *No,* he says, *I've seen this dog—Blue Daisy—walking around town, but I don't know who she belongs to.*

Wow—that dog has a name now. And we're the ones who gave it to her.

Sort of.

Here, Blue Daisy, Sam calls softly.

Blue Daisy tilts her head to look at him. Then she turns and walks away.

Come back, Blue Daisy, I call in a louder voice, but she trots off across the grass, over a hill, out of sight.

HAVE YOU SEEN BLUE DAISY?

SAM

*Katie, let's see if Blue Daisy stopped to drink
the water we put out,* I say when we get close to my
house. *Yes!* she says. *The bowl is empty! Do you think*

she knows we're the ones who put it there?
We look around, but we don't see Blue Daisy
anywhere. Instead we see—the Tracy twins. Where

did they come from? They ride by and shout,
Have you seen Blue Daisy? How do they know
her name? What do they care about

her? I shrug—I don't have to answer.
Why would I help them find Blue Daisy
just so they can throw things at her?

A PERFECTLY GOOD SOUP BONE

KATIE

We go to my house, and I cannot believe what I am seeing. Right outside the back door, my mom, who always says she does not like dogs, is about to give Blue Daisy a bath.

This dog, she says, *has been hanging around the yard for half an hour. Is this the one you've been talking about?*

Yes, I say.

Well, it sure is dirty, says Mom.

She's dragged a washtub outdoors and filled it up with water from the hose. She has a washcloth and a big old towel. Blue Daisy is standing off to the side, watching. *You wait there,* Mom says to her. *I'll be right back.*

She goes inside and comes out with a kettle of boiling water, adds that to the water in the tub, and sloshes it around. The whole time she's doing all this, Blue Daisy *does* wait there.

Okay, it's nice and warm now—come here, she says. She holds out a dog biscuit, and Blue Daisy trots over to get it.

Where did that come from? I ask Mom.

I bought some at the store this morning, she says.

My mouth drops open, but no words come out.

Mom pets Blue Daisy's neck and back, talking to her as she lifts her into the tub: *Where did you come from? How did you get this paint all over yourself? You're a good dog.*

Mom keeps talking as she washes her. And Blue Daisy seems to enjoy the whole thing.

It turns out Blue Daisy isn't gray, she's a beautiful light tan.

Mom rubs the flower gently, and a little bit of the paint comes off, but most of it is still there. She hands me the towel and lifts Blue Daisy out of the tub.

You two can dry her off, she says to Sam and me.

Blue Daisy backs away when we go near her. She shakes herself dry and sticks close to Mom.

Mom says, *That's strange. I wonder why she doesn't like towels.*

I don't look at Sam. But we know: it isn't towels that Blue Daisy doesn't like—it's us.

Mom rests her hand on Blue Daisy's ribs and says the most surprising thing yet: *Katie, why don't you go inside and get that soup bone out of the refrigerator.*

Out of the refrigerator? Not out of the garbage? She must mean the bone she was going to use to make soup.

I find the bone and bring it out, and just to make sure, I ask, *This is for Blue Daisy?*

Of course it is, says Mom. *Unless you want to chew on*

it. *And you don't need to tell your father that we gave a perfectly good soup bone to a hungry dog. What he doesn't know won't hurt him.*

As we watch Blue Daisy trot off with her bone, Mom says, *Did I hear you call that dog Blue Daisy? I've been wondering what we should call her.*

JUST THE SPOT

SAM

Now that Blue Daisy is nice and clean,
she starts making friends in the neighborhood—
even the Wilson sisters! Katie and I have never seen

them let a dog go near their flower bed,
but when Blue Daisy walks into their yard
with her bone, tall Ms. Wilson, instead

of yelling, *Shoo! Scram! Git out of here!,*
speaks gently: *I hear you have a name now.*
Well, Blue Daisy, I don't want you near

our impatience, but if you want to settle down
and chew on that bone, I know just the spot.
Blue Daisy follows her around,

not stepping on a single flower.
Then short Ms. Wilson actually *smiles*—first
at Blue Daisy and then at us! She asks, *How are*

you two doing? And then: *Chew on your bone*
as long as you like, Blue Daisy. I'll show you
a good place to bury it when you're done.

I. M. P. A. T. I. E. N. S.

KATIE

I think I might have figured something out.

When I go home for lunch, I ask Mom, *Is there some kind of flower named impatience?*

She thinks a minute and says, *Impatiens?* She spells it—I.M.P.A.T.I.EN.S.—and tells me the flowers are usually pink or white. *The Wilson sisters love that kind of flower,* she says. *Their garden is full of them. Why do you want to know?*

I'm not sure I should tell her. It might make her mad to hear that Sam and I have been in the Wilson sisters' garden. *Well,* I say, *they're always telling us kids not to trample their impatiens, and I thought it meant they were, you know—impatient—but then tall Ms. Wilson let Blue Daisy lie right down beside some other flowers, and told her to be careful not to go near her impatiens. And she pointed at some pink and white flowers. So that's why I wondered.*

Mom looks at me carefully. *You and Sam stay out of the Wilson sisters' yard. And keep that dog out too.*

I mean, she says more gently, *try to keep Blue Daisy out of places where she might get into trouble.*

Blue Daisy is the first dog my mom has ever liked.

A DOG BED

SAM

Blue Daisy must think she's in dog heaven,
in the Wilson sisters' garden with her bone,
but where will she go tonight? At seven

thirty, when it starts getting dark out,
we'll all have nice warm beds, but where will
Blue Daisy sleep? I can't stop thinking about

her. *Dad*, I ask, *is it okay if I use our old green
sleeping bag for a dog bed?* He says, *Good idea, Sam.
Blue Daisy can sleep here—the forecast is for rain*

tonight. I find the sleeping bag, shake
it, fold it, and put it on the back porch. Before
I go out looking for Blue Daisy, I make

sure to put fresh water by her bed. If I
can get Blue Daisy to sleep at our house tonight,
maybe Dad will let me keep her. It's worth a try.

OUR DOG NOW

KATIE

I don't see Sam all afternoon because I have to go to the dentist, and then Mom stops on the way home to get something for supper, since she gave that soup bone to Blue Daisy.

But right after supper Sam comes over to tell me, *Dad said Blue Daisy can sleep on our porch tonight. Only—where is she?*

We try calling her name all over the neighborhood.

Tall Ms. Wilson says, *She left here about an hour ago, heading in the direction of the park.* Short Ms. Wilson adds, *I saw the Tracy twins chasing her on their bikes.*

When we get to the park, there they are, and there's Blue Daisy with them! Did I just see Michael throwing stones at her?

Wait—I can't tell if they are chasing her, or if Blue Daisy is following them.

They're all the way across the park. We call out in our loudest voices, *Here, Blue Daisy!* She stops and glances over at us, but then she trots off after *them.*

They turn and ride toward us, and Blue Daisy stays right with them. When they get close, Miranda yells, *Looks like Blue Daisy is our dog now!*

No way! They don't even like her! I try calling Blue Daisy again, but she ignores me and runs after Michael and Miranda.

Then we see her eating something that they're throwing. *It's like Hansel and Gretel,* says Sam. *They're tricking Blue Daisy into going to their house!*

BLUE DAISY AND THE TRACY TWINS

SAM

Katie, I ask, *what are they feeding her? Blue
Daisy is following them and gobbling it all up.*
This time, she does not slip through

a hedge to get away. We watch her
trotting right along beside Miranda's bike,
as if Miranda is her new best friend. I sure

hope those two don't hurt her, but they might!
If she came to my house, she'd have a bed
waiting for her! We watch awhile, then lose sight

of Blue Daisy and the Tracy twins. Katie says, *Do you
think we should keep following them, Sam?*
I'm not sure—we don't actually own Blue

Daisy. But we keep going, all the way up the hill
to Michael and Miranda's house, staying out of view
because you never know what the Tracy twins will

do. When we get near their house, we hide behind
a big tree and peek around it. Whoa—this
is *not* what we thought we would find.

IT MIGHT RAIN

KATIE

Sam and I see Michael and Miranda sitting on their front steps. In front of them, Blue Daisy is lapping up a big bowl of dog food.

When she's finished, she leans her head on Michael's knee, and he turns to Miranda and says in a surprised voice, *I think Blue Daisy likes me.*

He slowly puts out his hand and touches the flower, and then runs two fingers down the stem that goes along her back.

Is Blue Daisy smiling?

I can't tell for sure. It's starting to get dark, and it looks like it might rain. Sam whispers, *Katie, we better go home.*

We leave before Michael and Miranda see us.

ONLY A TINY BIT

SAM

It's raining hard and I can't get to sleep.
Blue Daisy should be my dog! Or maybe Katie's.
We're the ones who like her best. I keep

thinking how she wouldn't have
a name if we hadn't painted a daisy on her back.
I made her a dog bed, and Mom let me save

a whole hamburger for her. Now
she won't even get one little bite.
The Tracy twins! I don't see how

she could choose them instead of us. It
isn't fair—they're the meanest kids in . . . Sure we
put some paint on her. But only a tiny bit.

HOME

Blue Daisy walks with her head held high.
She has enough food. She's clean and dry.
Everyone likes her and treats her well.
Whose dog is she? That's hard to tell.

WAS IT SAM?

KATIE

Mom made pancakes for breakfast, which I usually love, but I'm not hungry.

Katie, why aren't you eating? she asks. *Are you still fretting about Blue Daisy?*

I hate the word "fretting," and I hate how Mom can guess things. What would she say if she knew the whole truth about how Blue Daisy got her flower and her name?

Maybe I should confess before she figures it out.

Mom, I say, *if I tell you something, will you promise not to get mad?*

Big mistake. *What?* she says, without promising anything.

Well, I begin, *it's about Blue Daisy.*

She stares at me. *Do you know who painted that flower on her back?* And then, when I don't answer, she asks, *Was it Sam?*

Boy, do I want to say yes.

Not exactly, I answer.

Well? Mom says. And now I can't get out of this.

DIDN'T YOU TELL HER?

SAM

I walk over to Katie's house, trying
to figure out how we can get Blue Daisy back,
and I find Katie sitting on her steps crying!

What happened? I ask. She's so upset she
can barely talk. She crosses her arms. *Sam,*
she says, *I admitted to Mom that I painted the*

flower on Blue Daisy, and you should have heard
her: "Katie, that is so mean! I'm ashamed of you."
It's like nothing else counts. The baby bird

I rescued, or the cat and its kittens I fed
when they came to our yard, or—remember
the time I found that lady's injured dog and led

it back to her? I remember that—the lady gave
Katie a reward, and she donated all of it to the
animal rescue center. *You're always trying to save*

lost or injured animals, I say. *How could your own mom*
be ashamed of you? Katie sucks in her breath.
I know, she says. She calms down, but there's some

part of what she said that bothers me.
The whole time she was talking, she kept saying
"I"—I never heard her say "we."

Didn't you tell her, I ask, *that it was my
idea in the first place?* Katie shakes her head.
No, Sam, she says, *even if you thought of it, I*

*didn't say a word to stop you. And besides, you
only painted one line. I painted that whole flower.
Maybe it started out as your idea, but it's my fault too.*

SAM KICKS IT BACK

KATIE

Sam and I go to his house to put fresh water in the water bowl. We leave it on his porch beside the bed Blue Daisy didn't sleep in, and then we go looking for her.

What if she's still at Michael and Miranda's house? I ask.

They might tie her up to keep her there, says Sam.

We'd have to sneak into their yard and untie her, I say.

Even if they threw rocks at us? says Sam.

We'd have to risk it, I say. *But—maybe they wouldn't. Remember how Michael was petting Blue Daisy last night?*

Sam nods. *I don't know, Katie. That's the first time I've ever seen either of them act nice.*

We gather our courage as we approach their house. Miranda and Michael are kicking a ball back and forth in the street.

Hey, says Sam, puffing himself up, *I came to get my dog.*

Miranda stops the ball by stomping her foot on top of it. *What do you mean,* your *dog?* she demands. *Blue Daisy doesn't even like you.*

Sam un-puffs a little bit. That was a stab to the heart.

I come to his defense: *Yeah, she does. Blue Daisy loves Sam.*

Like I said—Sam jumps back in—*I came to get Blue Daisy. So, where is she?*

Michael looks at us for a minute and finally admits, *We don't know. She was gone when we got up this morning.*

Oh.

Sam and I look around their yard. We don't see a rope.

Miranda kicks the ball to Michael, ignoring us. I don't know what to say, and it seems like Sam doesn't either. We stand there for a minute.

Then Michael kicks the ball to me. I kick it over to Miranda, who kicks it at Sam. Sam kicks it back to Michael.

WHAT—TOGETHER?

SAM

We pass the ball around for a while.
I'm not sure what to do next. I glance
at Katie. She gives Michael half a smile

and says, *We better go now—Sam and I should
keep on looking for Blue Daisy.* They don't answer
until we start to leave. Then Michael says, *We could*

all look for her. Miranda makes a face and goes,
What—together? Michael says, *Why not?*
Miranda looks us over. *Well,* she says, *I suppose*

we might find her quicker that way. The four
of us stand there in the street. It's awkward.
Finally Katie says, *Sam?* And I say, *Sure.*

TREATING HER BETTER

KATIE

Sam, Michael, Miranda, and I start walking toward the park.

If I knew who put paint all over Blue Daisy, Miranda says, *I'd paint* them *and see how* they *like it.*

I glance at Sam. Does she suspect that it was us?

Well, you have to admit, I say, *it looks okay. Plus people are treating her better now that she has that flower.*

And a name, Sam adds.

Miranda gives Sam and me a long, hard look. *Yeah, but whoever did it didn't know any of that stuff would happen, did they?* she says.

I look down at the ground and keep walking.

Michael and Miranda are the mean ones, I remind myself.

Sam and I are nice.

BLUE DAISY'S BARK

SAM

Just before we get to the park
we all stop at the same time, listening.
That sounds like Blue Daisy's bark!

says Katie. *Something's wrong. I bet
she's hurt,* says Michael. The sound is coming from
the playground. We all start running. When we get

there, we see Blue Daisy—way up on top
of the climbing structure, looking down the slide.
She starts to put out a paw, then comes to a stop

and steps back. She looks scared. *How did she get so far
up that thing all by herself?* Michael asks. *Wait—look!*
He points to three teenagers running to their car

and laughing. Miranda says, *I bet they lifted her
up onto the platform and left her there!* It's hard
to believe, but it's probably true. Why else were

they running away like that? I don't want
to waste time thinking about them—we have to
get Blue Daisy down. But how? We can't

force her down the slide. The four of us try
to coax her, but she won't budge. Katie pats the slide.
Come on, Blue Daisy, she says. Then, to Miranda, *Why*

don't you climb up there and try to help her down?
Miranda climbs up and gently pets Blue Daisy. *Katie,*
she says, *you come up too. It's hard to do this on my own.*

Katie goes up and says, *Sam, stay there and be ready*
to catch her if we can get her to go down the slide.
Katie and Miranda hold Blue Daisy steady

and try to nudge her forward, but she
keeps stepping back. Then Michael says, *I have*
an idea. Maybe she'll come down if we

put these on the slide. He takes some black things
out of his pocket—what are they? Chunks of coal?
He puts some at the bottom of the slide and flings

a few up to the top. One hits Katie in the head.
Ow! she yells. *Why are you throwing things at us?*
Michael smiles up at her and says, *When we fed*

these to Blue Daisy, she followed us home. Maybe they will
help. Sure enough, Miranda holds out a chunk
and Blue Daisy turns her head and swallows it like a pill.

Katie and Miranda stay behind Blue Daisy
so there's no place for her to go but down. Michael
puts a few more chunks on the slide, and that crazy

dog slides down, right into my arms. Miranda follows,
and then Katie. We all end up in a big laughing heap
at the bottom of the slide. Blue Daisy chews and swallows

a whole handful of the chunks Michael gives her. *What
are those things?* I ask, and Michael answers, *Broken pieces
of burned snickerdoodles.* I should have thought of that!

AN APOLOGY?

KATIE

The five of us—four smiling kids and a happy dog—walk partway home together, and when we get to where Michael and Miranda go one way and Sam and I go another, I try to get Blue Daisy to come with us. But she doesn't. She follows them.

I ask Sam to come to my house for lunch. Mom might be nicer if he's there. When we get home, she makes us sandwiches and then starts to cut up apples. I can tell by the way she chops the apples that she's still thinking about this morning.

As soon as we sit down to eat, she says: *Sam, you must have seen what Katie did to that poor dog. Maybe you even helped her.* We both stop eating and look at Mom.

Is she going to say she's ashamed of Sam too?

Then she surprises us. *I was harsh this morning, Katie, and I'm sorry. I know you're not a mean person— and neither are you, Sam.*

But you two, she goes on, *owe Blue Daisy an apology.*

Sam glances at me. We know she's right. But how do you apologize to a dog? Especially one that won't come near you.

WE KNEW BETTER

SAM

Sam, Katie asks, *is painting Blue Daisy the worst
thing you've ever done*? I don't like that question,
because I did something on the last day of first

grade that I don't want to tell her about.
Probably, I answer. *But anyway, we know
better now.* We're sitting on the grass, out

in back, near where we painted her. *True,*
says Katie, but she doesn't leave it at that.
She looks straight at me. *We knew*

better when we did it, Sam. Two gray birds
tilt their heads as if they're listening. Apologizing
to Blue Daisy might take more than words.

DON'T RUB TOO HARD

KATIE

Sam and I decide to walk to the twins' house, and sure enough, there's Blue Daisy, running after a stick Miranda threw.

Hey, I say to Michael.

Hi, Katie. Hi, Sam, he says.

Do you have any more of those burned snickerdoodles? Sam asks.

Michael reaches into his pocket, takes one out, and breaks it into chunks. *Here,* he says. *She likes it if you hold them out and wait for her to come and get them.*

Sam sits down on their front steps, holding the chunks of snickerdoodle in his outstretched hand. I sit beside him. For a while nothing happens.

Then Miranda stops throwing the stick, and Blue Daisy looks at Sam, walks over to him, sniffs his hand, and accepts his offering.

I look at the flower on Blue Daisy's back. A little more of it has worn off, but you can still tell it's a daisy if you know it's supposed to be one.

Blue Daisy doesn't like that painted flower, says Miranda.

I touch the flower and then run my hand along Blue Daisy's neck and back.

We tried to get it off with soap and water, says Sam, *but that didn't work—do you have any other ideas?*

Miranda thinks about that. *Maybe you could brush it out,* she says.

I guess we could try, I say, *if we had the right kind of brush.*

Sam adds, *And if Blue Daisy would let us.*

Michael goes inside and comes back out with a brush that's partly soft and partly stiff. He gives it to me, saying, *Here, try this—don't rub too hard, or you might hurt her.*

Thanks, I say. I hold out the brush, and Blue Daisy doesn't run away. But before I brush her, I have something to say that I don't want anyone but her and Sam to hear.

Blue Daisy, I say softly. She turns toward my voice and tilts her head. I lean close to her ear and whisper, *Sam and I are sorry.*

And then she puts her head on my knees and lets me brush her fur. I'm as careful as I was with the paint-brush. Maybe she remembers.

Maybe she forgives me.

Petal by petal, the flower disappears.

I give the brush to Sam and he brushes away the stem.

Blue Daisy, he says when he's finished, *I have a bed for you at my house. On the back porch, where it's cool on hot nights and warm on cold nights.*

Miranda says, *We were thinking she could stay here.*

Michael adds, *At least some of the time.*

Blue Daisy looks around at the four of us. She cocks her head, and I get an idea.

Sam, could we all sleep on your porch tonight?

Sure, he says.

It might be the first time I've seen Miranda smile.

Michael is looking at Blue Daisy, admiring how she looks now—not quite so skinny, and with a nice clean back.

Blue Daisy, he says, *you can sleep wherever you want.*

Blue Daisy wags her tail and gives us a big dog smile.

After supper, Sam and I go back to help Michael and Miranda bring their things to Sam's house.

Let's go past Mr. Jenkins' house, says Miranda. *Have you noticed that when he burns a batch of cookies, he tries again a few days later?*

I have noticed that—and it turns out we're right. Mr. Jenkins is in his yard when we go by. *Wait here a minute,* he says.

He goes in and comes back out with a plate of oatmeal macaroons. As he's passing them around, a young man and woman walk by. They were there when Blue Daisy got her name, and they remember her.

Hello, Blue Daisy, says the woman.

Looking good, says the man.

Mr. Jenkins gives them each a cookie, and they walk away—holding hands, I notice. Mr. Jenkins passes the plate around again.

He takes something out of his pocket and offers it to Blue Daisy. She sniffs at it and looks up at him, as if to ask, *What's this?*

She sure likes those snickerdoodles the way you make them, Michael says.

Mr. Jenkins laughs and scratches Blue Daisy behind her ears. *Well, my friend,* he says, *it's probably not good for you to eat too many of those. I made these dog biscuits just for you.* He even used a special cookie cutter, so they're shaped like bones.

Blue Daisy gobbles up a dog biscuit and trots off down the street. Mr. Jenkins says, *Don't worry, she'll be back.*

He gives us three dog biscuits each. *I know they look good enough to eat,* he says, *but you kids eat the macaroons I made for you and save those to give to Blue Daisy later.*

We put them in our pockets and go to Sam's house, where we fill Blue Daisy's bowl with fresh water and put one dog biscuit on each step.

Michael says, *Let's put a few more on the ground in front of the steps to lead her to the other ones.*

After we do that, we arrange our four sleeping bags around Blue Daisy's bed. We stay up late talking, trying not to fall asleep before she finds us.

Miranda says, *I wonder where Blue Daisy is.*

And right then, Sam sits up straight and says, *Listen!*

We hear dog steps and the sound of sniffing.

GOOD NIGHT. WOOF. GOOD NIGHT.

SAM

We are all immediately wide-awake—
it's her! We scramble around, clearing the way
for her to join us. *Come on in*, I say. *Make*

yourself at home, Blue Daisy. She takes a drink,
eats her treats, and finds her bed, then turns three times
and settles down. Katie says, *No matter what we think,*

Blue Daisy belongs to herself. Michael says, *Right*
now, she's here with us. And that's enough. We all agree.
Good night. Good night. Woof. Good night. Good night.

EPILOGUE
ONE YEAR LATER

Sometimes people new to town ask how
Blue Daisy got her name. By now,
we all skip to where the story ends:
Blue Daisy was named by her four best friends.

RECIPES

MR. JENKINS'
SNICKERDOODLES

(Be sure to get an adult to help you.)

Get out all the ingredients before you start, so you'll have everything you need. This recipe makes about 80 cookies.

INGREDIENTS

1 cup butter or margarine
  (or ½ cup of each),
  soft but not melted

1½ cups sugar

2 eggs

1 teaspoon vanilla

2¾ cups flour

3 teaspoons baking powder

½ teaspoon salt

4 more tablespoons sugar

1 tablespoon cinnamon

DIRECTIONS

Preheat the oven to 400° F.

Using an electric mixer, mix the butter (or margarine) and the 1½ cups of sugar together until the mixture is light and fluffy.
Add the eggs and mix again.
Add the vanilla and mix again.
These are the "wet ingredients."

In a separate bowl, mix the flour, baking powder, and salt. If you have a flour sifter, sift them together. Otherwise, stir with a spoon to be sure they are well mixed.
These are the "dry ingredients."

Add the dry ingredients to the wet ingredients, about ¼
at a time, mixing after each addition.

In a separate small bowl, mix the 4 tablespoons of sugar and
1 tablespoon of cinnamon.

For each cookie, scoop up a spoonful of dough and shape it
into a ball about the size of a walnut. Roll each ball around
in the cinnamon-sugar mixture until it is completely covered.
Place the balls about two inches apart on a cookie sheet—
they will flatten and spread out. (You don't need to grease the
cookie sheet before putting the balls of cookie dough on it.)

Bake for 8 minutes.

Take the cookie sheet out of the oven and move the cookies
to a cooling rack. When they are cool, put them in airtight
containers to keep them fresh.

Blue Daisy likes dog biscuits better than snickerdoodles, and
they are better for her too, so use the next recipe if you want
to make treats for your favorite dog.

MR. JENKINS'
DOG BISCUITS

(Be sure to get an adult to help you.)

Get out all the ingredients before you start, so you'll have everything you need. You can add other ingredients like cornmeal or bacon bits if you know your dog will like them. This recipe will make about 40 two-inch biscuits.

INGREDIENTS

2 cups whole wheat flour (plus a little more for dusting the surface when you roll out the dough)

¼ cup rolled oats

2 large eggs

¼ cup oil (Safflower oil is a good kind of oil for dogs.)

½ cup water or chicken or beef stock (If the dough is too sticky, add a little more flour or rolled oats. If it's too stiff, add a little more water or stock.)

DIRECTIONS

Preheat the oven to 350° F.

Use your hands to mix all the ingredients in a bowl.

Mix well and shape the dough into two balls, each about the size of a softball.

Sprinkle some flour on a table or counter.

Put a ball of dough on the floured surface.

Roll the ball of dough in the flour so it isn't too sticky to handle or roll out. You may need to sprinkle a little more flour on the surface before you roll out the dough.

SHAPING THE BISCUITS

Use a rolling pin to roll out the dough so it's about ¼ inch thick.

Cut the biscuits into any shape. If you have a bone-shape cookie cutter, you can use that, but any shape will work. If you don't have a cookie cutter, you can cut the biscuits into two-inch squares.

If you don't have a rolling pin, make walnut-size balls of dough and flatten them with your hand or use the bottom of a glass to press them down.

BAKING

Spray a cookie sheet with cooking spray or rub it with any kind of oil or grease.

Place the biscuits on the baking sheet.

Bake for 20 minutes.

Take the cookie sheet out of the oven and let the biscuits cool.

After the biscuits have cooled, store them in an airtight container.

If you want them to last longer, keep them in the refrigerator or freezer.

AUTHOR'S NOTE

Sam tells his parts of the story in poems, while Katie's story is in prose. Do you know the difference?

Prose is written in sentences and paragraphs, following conventions such as:

The first line of each new paragraph is indented.

When people are talking, a new paragraph is used for each new speaker.

Poetry can take many different forms. It is written in lines with specific breaks and is sometimes separated into parts called stanzas. I composed Sam's poems in three-line stanzas, rhyming the last words of the first and third lines of each stanza. A few of the rhymes are half-rhymes, which means the rhyme is not exact.

In many books, speech is indicated by quotation marks around the spoken words. However, in this story, I have indicated speech with italics. I've chosen to do this because that is what I always do in poems, and I wanted Sam's poems and Katie's prose to be the same in that way.

I hope you enjoy reading—and writing—both prose and poetry!

ACKNOWLEDGMENTS

Thank you:

Margaret Ferguson, and everyone at Holiday House

Ginger Knowlton, and everyone at Curtis Brown

Early readers: Lissa, Christine, and Kenna Howe; Amy, Lizzie, and Emma Jayne Knorr; Ashley, Annabelle, Jack, and Addy Simpson; Anne Bartlett and Jem, Naima, and Teo van Tyn

Very early encouragers: J. Patrick Lewis and Doreen Rappaport

Society of Children's Book Writers and Illustrators, with special thanks to Indiana SCBWI and the Fort Wayne critique group

And always, my home team: Chad, Lloyd and Anastacia (and Peanut and Olive), and Glen